P9-CQL-417

If I Built a School

Chris Van Dusen

DIAL BOOKS FOR YOUNG READERS

HA
CASS COUNTY PUBLIC LIBRARY
400 E. MECHANIC
HARRISONVILLE, MO 64701

0 0022 0558600 7

Jack, on the playground, said to Miss Jane,

This school is OK, but it's pitifully plain.

The builder who built this I think should be banned.

It's nothing at **all** like the school I have planned.

If I built a school, the first thing you'd meet

Are lots of cute puppies! They'd flock to your feet!

But why stop at puppies? Why not a whole zoo?

So I'd add a bunch of big animals too!

Right off the lobby, to get to your class,

I'd set up a system of tubes made of glass.

You hop in a pod, press the number, then ZOOM!

In under ten seconds, you're right at your room!

All of the classrooms are built onto towers

That sprout from the schoolyard like colorful flowers.

And like giant petals that welcome the day,

The roofs open up in a similar way.

Panels fold back and they let in the sun,

Which frankly makes being there that much more fun.

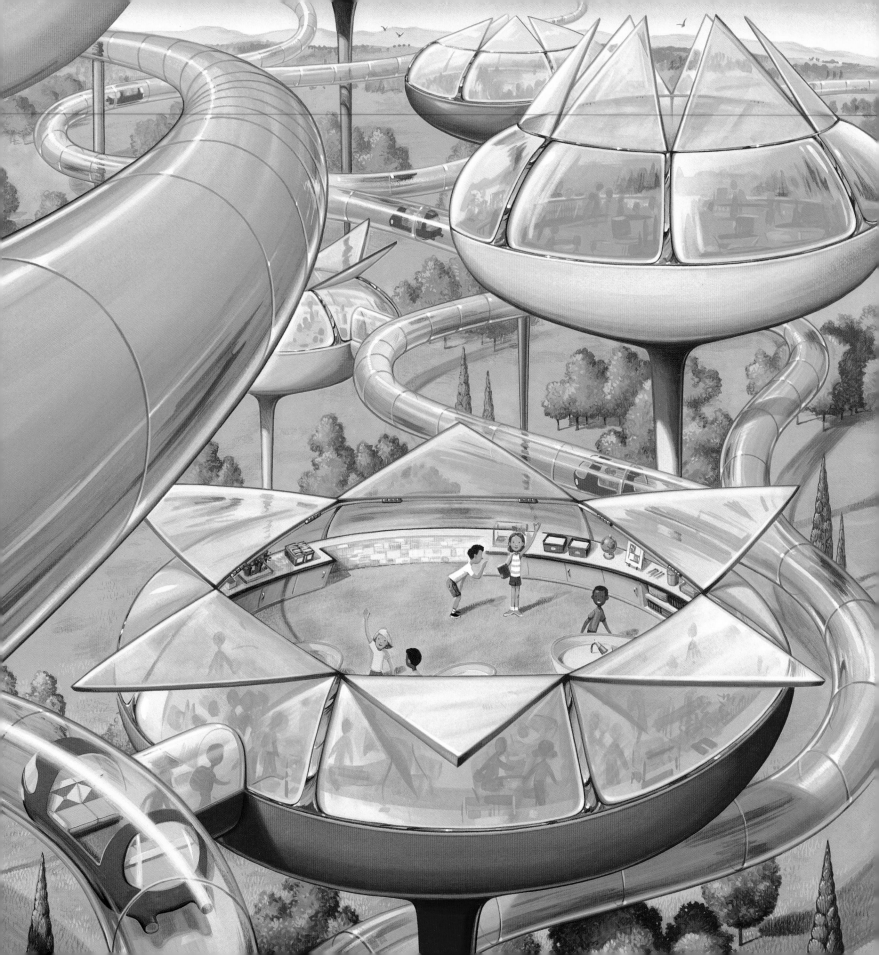

Now come see your **classroom**. Isn't it grand?

That free-floating platform is where you would stand.

And using a stylus, you write in the air.

No blackboard. No whiteboard. No, nothing is there.

Your words just appear and they magically glow.

(Don't ask how this works 'cause I don't really know.)

But you're not the only one floating around.

Check out the desks. They don't touch the ground!

These are my **hover desks**. See how they glide?

They even have bumpers in case you collide.

In my kind of classes, we wouldn't have tests.
I'd liven things up with some hologram guests!
Here are some samples of what I've been thinkin'—
You might meet a T. rex or Abraham Lincoln!

The library's next, so let's have a look.

You won't find your everyday regular book.

These books come alive when removed from the racks.

They pop up like pop-ups, but pop to the max!

And if you're not sure what a book is about,

You'll find out quite quickly when something pops out!

It's off to the gym, and this place is so cool!
Around it, please note my perimeter pool.
The pool's a deep oval that everyone likes—
You race underwater on submarine bikes!
Up there is my trampoline basketball court.
It's partly a bounce house and partly a sport.
There's also a rock wall, and here's something new:
I've added some skydiving wind tunnels too!

I just heard the lunch bell, so let's go and eat.
I'd like you to meet my new robo-chef, Pete.
He's twenty feet tall and he spins on a gear.
You order your lunch in this microphone here.
And Pete can make anything, simple or weird—
From PB & jelly to squid, lightly seared.

It's now time for recess. Let's head out the door.

My **playground** is awesome! So much to explore!

Fly on the zip line way up in the sky,

Or slide down the twisty slide three stories high.

And after all that, if you're hot and you're beat,

Then you can go tubing. Now *that* would be sweet!

In **art** we use sprayers to splash out the paint.

In **music** we're LOUD, but our teacher's a saint.

And over in **science**, just one of the features

Is lab-grown genetically modified creatures!

We'll visit new places! Travel! Explore!

'Cause we'll go on field trips—field trips galore!

My specialty **buses** will tote us around.

They dive underwater! They blast off the ground!

And yes, they have wheels like our regular cars,

Which neatly retract when we rocket to Mars!

My school will amaze you. My school will astound.

By far the most fabulous school to be found!

Perfectly planned and impeccably clean.

On a scale, 1 to 10, it's more like 15!

And learning is fun in a place that's fun too.

If I built a school, that's **just** what I'd do!

This book is dedicated to my brother, Glenn,

who is the most naturally talented and gifted teacher I know.

DIAL BOOKS FOR YOUNG READERS

An imprint of Penguin Random House LLC, New York

Copyright © 2019 by Chris Van Dusen

Visit us at penguinrandomhouse.com

Penguin supports copyright. Copyright fuels creativity, encourages diverse voices, promotes free speech, and creates a vibrant culture. Thank you for buying an authorized edition of this book and for complying with copyright laws by not reproducing, scanning, or distributing any part of it in any form without permission. You are supporting writers and allowing Penguin to continue to publish books for every reader.

LIBRARY OF CONGRESS CATALOGING-IN-PUBLICATION DATA

Names: Van Dusen, Chris, author, illustrator. • Title: If I built a school / Chris Van Dusen.
Description: New York, NY : Dial Books for Young Readers, [2019] • Summary: Imaginative Jack describes the kind of school he would build—one full of animals, with tubes to transport students directly to their classrooms, and library books that come alive.
Identifiers: LCCN 2019008251 • ISBN 9780525552918 (hardback) • Subjects: • CYAC: Stories in rhyme. • Schools—Fiction.
Imagination—Fiction • BISAC: JUVENILE FICTION / School & Education. • JUVENILE FICTION / Imagination & Play.
JUVENILE FICTION./Art & Architecture. • Classification: LCC PZ8.3.V335 Ifs 2019 • DDC [E]—dc23
LC record available at https://lccn.loc.gov/2019008251

Printed in China   10 9 8 7 6 5 4

Designed by Jason Henry • Text set in Sixpack Regular and Avenir
The artwork for this book was created with gouache on cold press illustration board.